Charlie's Treasures

A story
By
Richard Neumann

Illustrations
By
Dian de Wolf

July, 2001

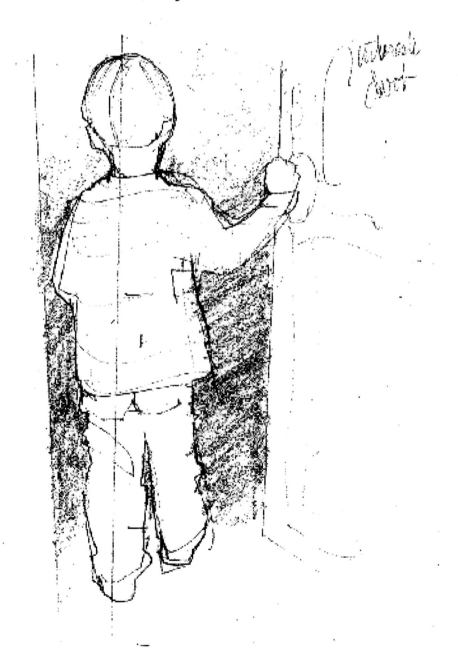

Printed by Global Ink, Inc.
Printed and bound in China

Stone In The Surf Press
PO Box 1063
Kenwood, CA 95452
www.richneumann.com

To God
Thanks for the Marbles

Special Thanks to Dean Morrissey
for his help and guidance

A tiny brass bell chimed as Charlie pushed open the door
to the shop. Clutched in the young boy's hand was a
worn leather pouch. Inside the shop it was dark, except
for a banker's light on top of an old roll top desk at the
very far end of the room. Charlie looked around and was
certain he was alone.

"Back here. By the light," a voice called out to him.

Charlie carefully navigated his way through the piles of odds and ends stacked everywhere. In the dim light he could see old pieces of pottery, books, paintings, rocks, toys, and tools. There was even one of those models of the solar system that spin when you turn a crank. Charlie stopped to admire it. He had always been fascinated by the intricate mechanism of tiny gears and chains that made it work.

"Take your time. Feel free to explore," the voice said.

Charlie continued on, walking carefully past a sundial sitting askew on top of its pedestal. There was so much to explore here. More toys, tools and treasures than he had ever seen before. Some he recognized and other things were beyond his imagination. A mobile of birds and flying machines hung from the ceiling, and an old toy steam train sat silent on its track. Next to the roll top desk was a Tyrannosaurus Rex that was almost as tall as he was. On the wall was a huge clock and on top of the pigeonholes lay a plush duckbilled platypus watching over the desk.

The old man set his glasses down, turned and smiled at the child. "Charlie," he said with a gleam in his voice. "It's been awhile."

"Please sit down," the old man said.

Charlie looked around. There were so many things stuffed and stacked everywhere that he could find no place to sit.

The old man cleared off the top of a large trunk and placed the items carefully on a wooden workbench behind him. "Sit." He patted the top of the trunk.

Charlie set the small bag he was holding on top of the trunk and hopped up. He wiggled until he was comfortable, then sat quietly dangling his legs in the air. He picked up the leather bag and held it in his hands.

The old man leaned forward and stroked his long white beard. "What do you have there?" He pointed to the bag Charlie was holding.

"Treasures," Charlie replied shyly.

The old man studied the bag carefully. "Treasures?"

"Yeah," said Charlie.

The old man leaned forward to get a closer look. "Hmm. Treasures in that tiny bag?"

Charlie held the bag tighter. "I've been collecting them all my life."

"You have?" The old man leaned back just a bit. "May I see them?"

Charlie held tight to the small bag and thought for a long time. These were his most valuable treasures. Finally, he nodded and untied the frayed strings that held the bag shut. He emptied the contents into his cupped hand.

The old man's eyes grew wide as he admired the treasures. "I have never seen such a marvelous collection of marbles before."

Charlie held his hands out so the old man could see his treasures better. "These aren't just marbles. Each one is a special treasure."

The old man carefully inspected the collection of marbles in Charlie's hand. "I see," he said with great interest. "Can you tell me about them?"

Charlie grinned from ear to ear with pride. "It will take a long time."

The old man smiled back. "For you, Charlie, I have all the time in the world."

"Each treasure has a name. That way you can tell them apart without having to describe them. It's much easier than having to say the one with the red, white and blue swirls."

"Very clever," the old man said as he studied the handful of marbles.

Charlie sorted through his treasures and carefully picked one. He held it up until it caught the light from the lamp on the desk. Deep colors shone through the swirls of glass. Charlie thought for a long time about this marble. "Like this one. This is Miller. I think this was the very first treasure I ever found. I've had it for a very long time. In fact, it's been with me since before kindergarten. If you look really hard, you can see it has a neat pattern deep inside. See?" He held it up.

The old man studied the swirls of colors. "I can see that and being the first makes it extra special."

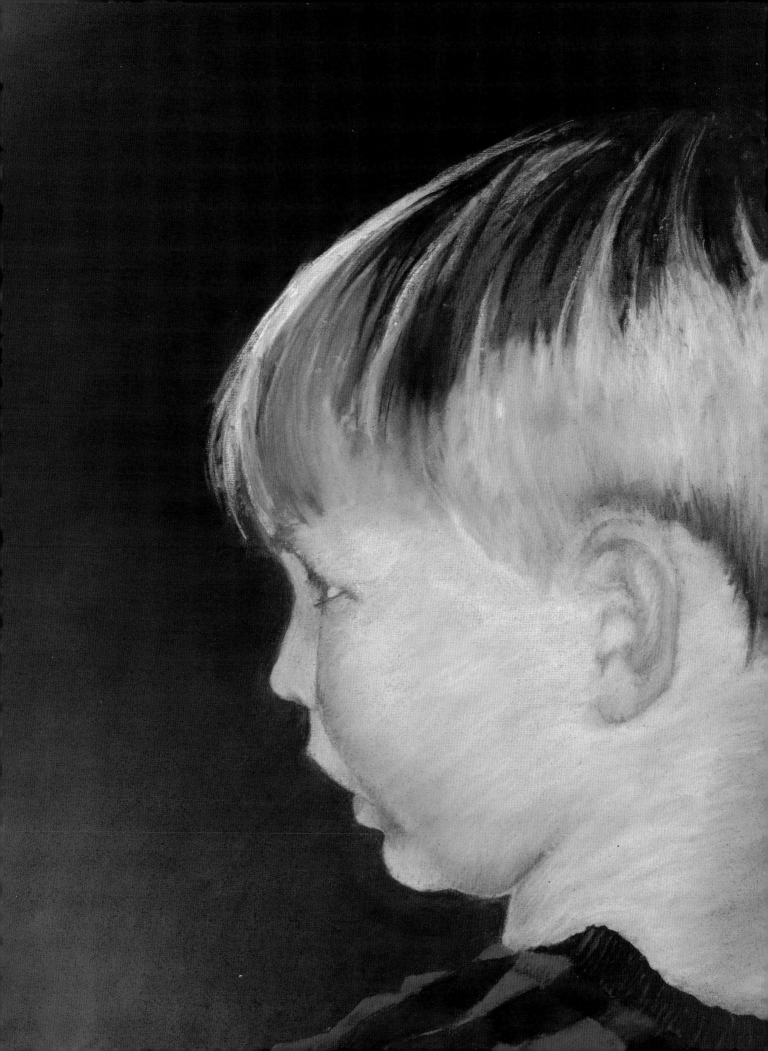

Charlie carefully placed Miller into the bag and selected a shiny metal marble. "This is Steely. That's because it's made of metal not glass. It's heavier and harder to control. But when you need a straight shooter, nothing beats it. Here."

Charlie placed the marble into the old man's hand. He held it carefully.

"Don't worry," Charlie assured him. "You can't break Steely, even if you dropped it or hit it really hard by mistake."

"I see," the old man said. He gave the marble a shine by rubbing it on his sleeve, then handed it carefully back to Charlie. "It's good to have a Steely in your collection."

Charlie chose another marble from his hand. He held it up until the light reflected off its smooth white surface. "See how it kind of glows? It's called a Moonie 'cause it looks like the moon at night when it's full. My mom says it has a special irr… irra…"

"Iridescence"

"Yeah, iridescence. This marble is very fragile. You can break them if you're not careful." He rotated the marble and pointed to a scuffed part on its surface. "See. I was playing around and hurt this one." Charlie looked at the scuffed spot and was very sad. "I don't know how to fix it."

The old man took the marble and rubbed the scuffed part with his thumb. The mark did not go away. He returned the marble to Charlie. "It's o.k. on the inside. Sometimes these marks just remind you that your treasures can be tougher than you think."

The next marble put a big grin on Charlie's face. "This is Latticinio. I always think it's dancing. Even when it's not moving, it looks like it's dancing. And every time I play with Latticinio I want to dance. I can't help but be happy. I like to think there's music trapped inside."

The old man took the marble and let it roll and dance in his palm. Then he held it up to his ear and listened carefully. Charlie watched in wonder as the old man's feet began to tap to the rhythm of a distant song. He handed the marble back to Charlie. "I love salsa music; it's so alive!"

Charlie laughed when he picked up the next treasure. "This is Lutz. Lutz the Klutz I call it."

"Lutz the Klutz?"

"Yeah. There's something about it that's a bit out of balance. It'll never go in a straight line. I'd line up a straight shot and old Lutz the Klutz would roll along. Then zing! Off he'd go in some weird direction. Some people wouldn't like that, but I look at it as a surprise in every roll."

"May I try?"

"Sure." Charlie handed Lutz the Klutz to the old man.

He rolled it on the wood floor and they watched as it zigged right, then zagged left. They both laughed. Charlie hopped off the trunk and picked Lutz up off the dusty wooden floor. Then he climbed back on top of the trunk.

"A good treasure," the old man said, "will always surprise you."

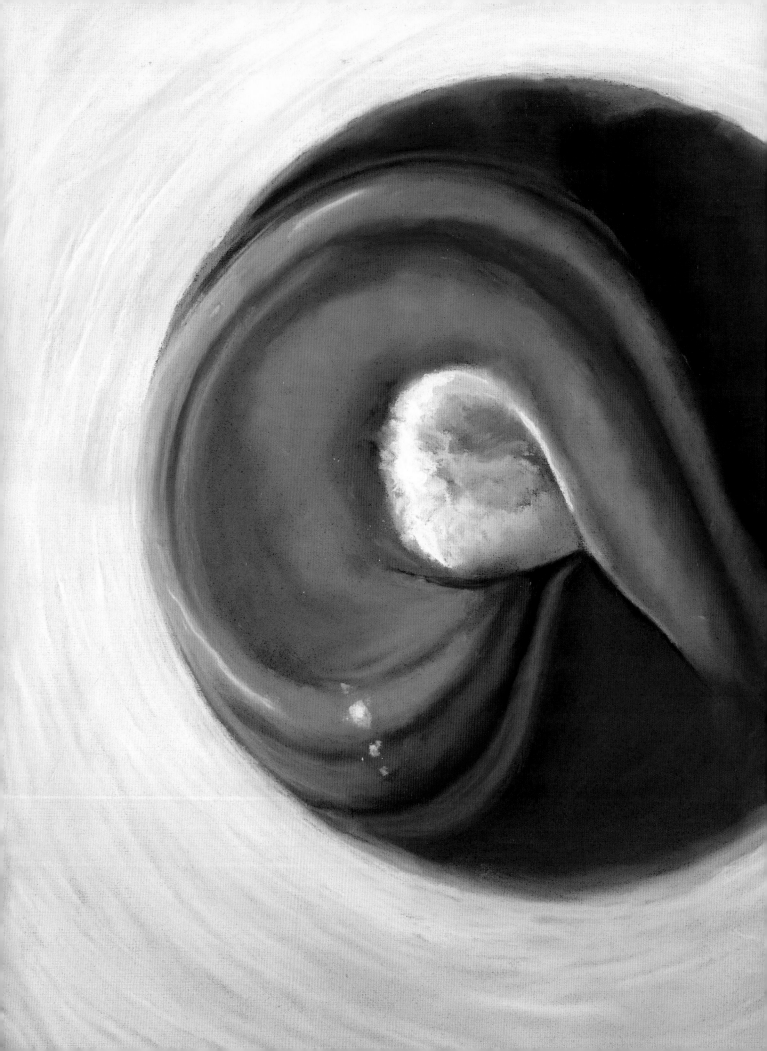

Charlie made his voice as deep as possible when he held up the next marble. "This is Slag," he said, as if he were announcing some great monster.

The old man drew back in pretend fear.

Charlie continued. "Slag is the biggest, meanest, toughest marble ever made!"

"Really?" The old man trembled.

"Nah! But it sure looks like it. Every once in a while you'd get surrounded in a game. But, I always knew I'd be o.k. when I pulled out Slag. See," he dropped the marble into the old man's hand, "just an ordinary marble, but it looks big and powerful. Slag and I won some good games together."

The old man returned Slag with great respect. "It's good to know the difference between how your treasure looks on the outside and what it truly is on the inside."

"Ready for this?" Charlie grinned. "This is Clambroth. I used to call it Clambreath."

The old man wrinkled his nose. "I know a clam's breath is very unpleasant."

"I know it was kind of mean, but the name stuck. When we'd play, I used to shout, 'look out, here comes Clambreath!' Even though I made up a rotten nick name, like Miller, Clambroth has been with me forever."

"Wonderful isn't it, how your treasures will stick by you."

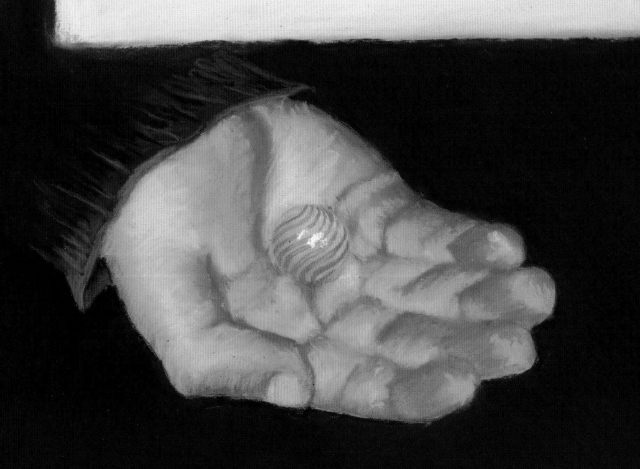

"This is Bennington. It's very old." Charlie held up a marble that was covered with chips and scratches. It had not been round for many years. "This was my dad's before me. When we had to move, I thought I had lost it. My dad was very sad."

"But you have it now."

"One day it just showed up. Out of nowhere! We were cleaning out the garage and, presto, there was old Bennington. I don't know who was happier, me or dad. Mom said it was a miracle."

The old man nodded his head. "It must have been. Quite a journey Old Bennington must have had to find you again."

Charlie chose a very special marble. "I got a chance to make a marble one time."

"You did?" The old man replied.

"This," he held the marble up high. "This is Robin.

"I am very impressed."

Charlie looked down. "I didn't do much really. I put in some ingredients and started them moving. Then all I could do is sit back and watch as the colors swirled and solidified. This is how it turned out."

The old man took the marble and held it gently in the palm of his hand. "It is a fine marble, Charlie. Very fine, indeed. Robin is filled with wonderful colors. And such depth! You must be very proud of this one."

"I am!" Charlie beamed. "I am."

Charlie held up a marble with deep swirls of dark and light. "Boy, did I screw up with this one. I traded Navarre for a bag of carnival glass. Thought I was being really smart. I didn't realize how rare this treasure was."

"This is a rare marble?"

"Yep. Only one like it."

"How did you ever get it back?"

Charlie remembered a special day. "I thought it was long gone. Then one day I was in this shop and there it was. I know this was my Navarre, 'cause it's the only one like it in the whole world. It cost me a lot, but I didn't care. It was worth it to get it back."

"Funny how that works out isn't it? Just when you least expect it, your treasures show up."

"Yeah. It's like they know somehow."

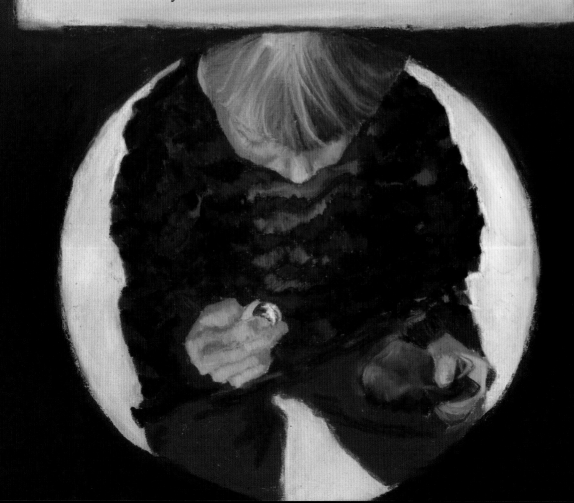

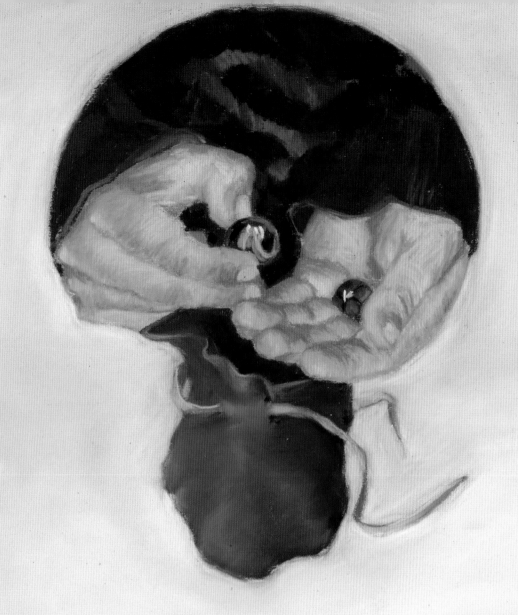

Charlie was down to his last two treasures. He picked up one with dark glass and deep swirls of color. "This is Pontil. I found it a couple of months ago. I thought the last thing I needed was another treasure." He shook his head. "I guess I was wrong."

"Why do you say that?"

"Well, I thought I had all of the treasures I'd ever want and I sort of lost interest in looking for new ones. But, Pontil just kind of showed up. I call it my thinker marble."

"A thinker?"

"Yeah. When I need to sort stuff out, I just look at Pontil. See." He held it up so that the old man could look into the marble. "Sometimes if you turn it just right and look deep inside, you can see yourself."

"The best treasures are like that."

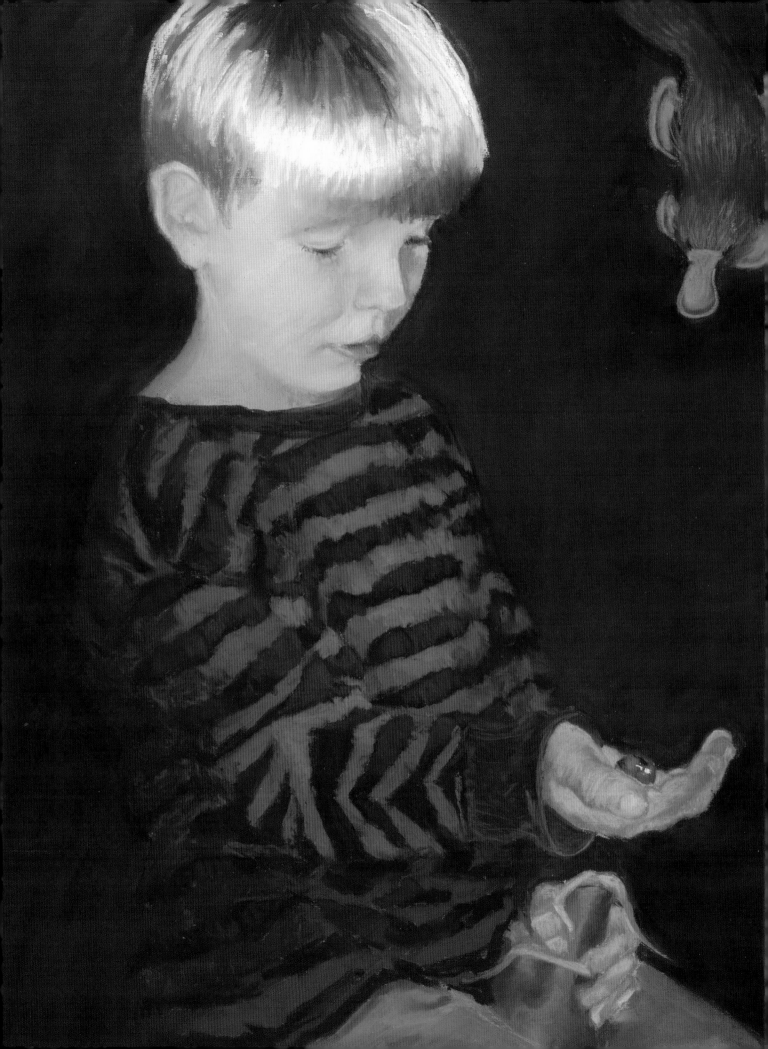

"I know this one very well," said the old man. "It's a cat's eye."

"I made up the nick name Cat for short." Charlie sat quietly and looked at the last marble in his hand.

"Are you o.k., Charlie?" the old man asked. He was very concerned.

"Yeah. I never realized how much I'd miss my treasures. I don't know what I'd do if I ever lost them, especially my Cat."

"Why?"

Charlie thought for a moment. "Because each one has been a special part of my life. And Cat," he paused. "Cat has been my best marble. I found it one day at one of those places filled with a zillion other marbles. My mom said I only could pick one, so I looked and looked. It seemed like forever. And then I found it! Somehow, I just knew this was the one marble I was looking for. Cat's been with me through all kinds of stuff. I even held it in my hand when I got really sick and had to go to the hospital. I'll never let go of it."

"Cat is a very special treasure, indeed. I can see that you have chosen all of your treasures very carefully." The old man took Charlie's hand in his. "Charlie, do you want to know something?"

"Sure."

"If you keep these treasures close to your heart, you'll never lose them and they will never lose you." He closed Charlie's fingers tightly around Cat and placed the boy's hand over his heart.

With his other hand, Charlie held the bag of marbles to his chest.

"And do you want to know something else?" The old man smiled.

"Sure," Charlie nodded.

"I have a treasure too?"

"You do? Can I see it?" Charlie was very curious.

"It would be an honor to share it with you." The old man reached deep into a pocket over his heart. Carefully, he pulled something out and held it in his closed hand. Slowly he opened his hand. In the old man's palm sat the most magnificent marble Charlie had ever seen. It glowed with a brilliance that almost hurt his eyes. He let Charlie look at it for a long time and then with a smile he said. "This is only one of the many treasures I have."

Charlie admired the marble. "What's it called?"

"Ah," the old man said with great pride. "What makes all of my treasures special, is that each one is unique. This one is named…. 'Charlie'."

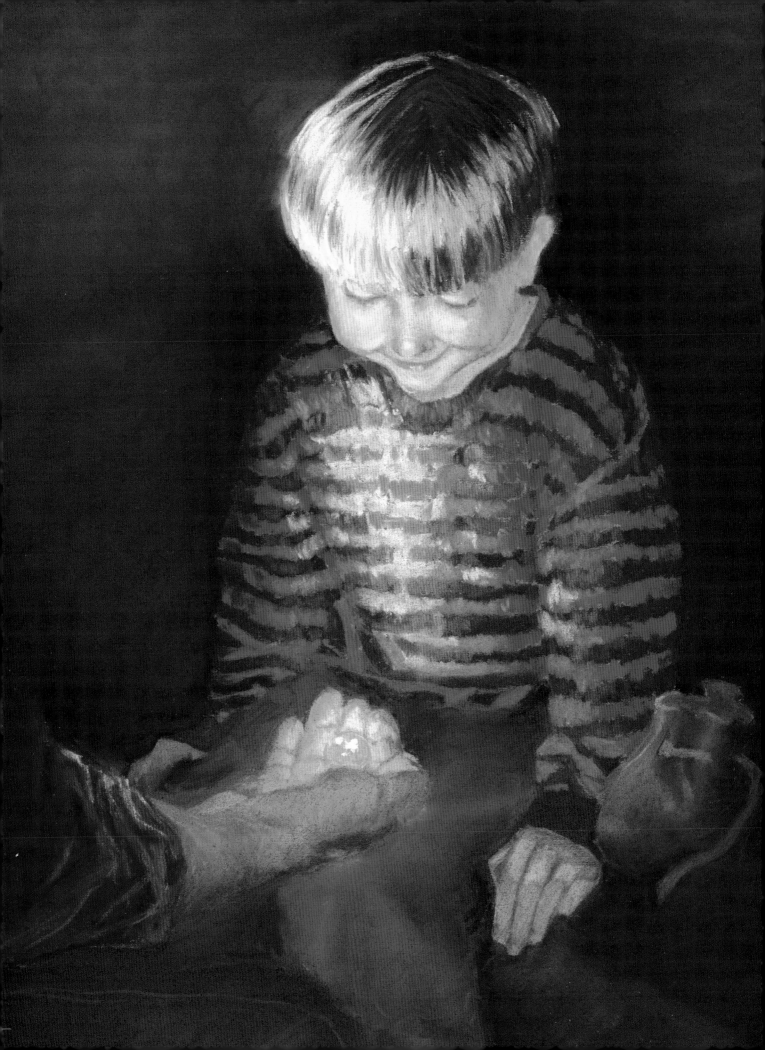

A Little Background On Charlie's Treasures

When I began this story, the image of a small boy and a bag of marbles was very clear in my mind. I can remember, as a boy playing with Moonies, Steelies and Cat's Eyes. I found it fascinating as I researched marbles for the story, that there are so many different types. Marbles have a rich and colorful history that is reflected in such names as; Root Beer Floats, Rainbos, Sunsets, Galaxies, and Bananas. There is a whole world out there of people who collect marbles. The study of marbles has even coined it's own name, mibology. A key factor in my selection was that each marble had to also be a real or probable name of a person. This story is not really about marbles, but about treasures. Interestingly enough, a Lutz sold recently for $6,000! My guess is that Charlie would never put a price on the value of Lutz the Klutz or any of his other treasures.

Richard Neumann

"When you hold a marble in your hand, you hold a piece of history."
-- Marilyn Barrett

"Miller"

This is one of the earliest marbles produced by a machine in the United States. They were manufactured by the Peltier Glass Company in Ottawa, Illinois. The company was founded in 1886. In the early 1920's an employee named Miller developed a machine for making marbles, thus the name Miller. The marbles are categorized as "slags" and have a translucent colored base mixed with white opaque swirls.

Miller is also a rather common name derived from the term Mill-wright, someone who runs a mill.

"Steely"

Steelies are, as their name implies, made from steel. They are generally large industrial ball bearings. These bearings must be perfectly round and made from the hardest metal.

Steely, although unusual, is also a surname.

"Latticinio"

These are some of the most common of the handmade marbles of the golden era of marbles in the 1920's and 1930's. Latticinios are named for the varied patterns of twisted colored glass that create a lattice pattern inside a clear marble. It may be a bit difficult to pronounce at first, but Latticinio has a very exotic sound to it.

The name seems to call from some far away South American country.

"Slag"

Slags refer to any number of marbles that are made by hand. A common feature of a slag is the pattern of opaque white formed as the glass was twisted as it was pulled from the furnace. This is known as the "nine and tail." Peltier, Akro Agate and M.F. Christensen were well known manufactures of slags.

Although I've never met the one Slag in the California phone book, I pictured a big guy with a heart of gold. The kind of friend you want to have around any time, especially in a jam.

"Ribbon Lutz Swirl"

Lutz is a terminology for glass marbles that contain very fine particles of mica or goldstone spangled throughout the glass.

Lutz also happens to be a surprisingly common name. It is also the name of the Olympic figure skater that had his signature routine named after him. I am almost certain that there is no relationship between the skater and Lutz the Klutz.

"Clambroth"

Clambroths are one of the more interesting of transitional marbles. It characterizes the shift between the handmade and machine made. Clambroths are easily identified by their milky white base and pinkish swirls.

I will confess that try as I might, there are no "Clambroths" listed in the U.S. or Canadain phone books. I thought the name was fun and somehow it just fit one of Charlie's friends.

"Moonie"

Flint Moonies, or more commonly known simply as Moonies, were produced by many different marble companies. Moonies are known for their white opalescent quality with hints of brown, red, blue and green. One of the most successful companies to produce Moonies was the Akro Agate Company, founded in 1910 in Akron, Ohio. They produced a wide variety of collectible marbles until unfortunate circumstances closed their doors in 1951.

Moonie, as a marble, is almost as rare as it is a name.

"Blue Bennington"

Benningtons are one of the few types of marbles made of porcelain clay instead of glass. They first appeared in Germany around 1870. Benningtons were also produced by two potteries in Ohio, which manufactured Benningtons in colors of brown (manganese) or blue (cobalt).

Bennington, I think, is a rather noble name and perfect for either a long-standing friend of the family or a marble.

"Robin"

Made by the Marble King company in the early 1950's, these blended marbles were never distributed to the public. It is uncertain why these marbles were never put into production. It is possible that these were accidents or the result of experimentation. What is certain is that these marbles are unique and surprisingly rich in their colors and patterns.

And much to my surprise, "Robin Marble" is also a rather common name.

"Navarre Transitional Slag"

Navarre Transitional Slags were made by the Navarre Glass Marble and Specialty Company, which, although founded in 1897, did not become a successful company until 1905 when it was purchased by M. F. Christensen. The company was located in Navarre, Ohio. Transitional refers to marbles that are partially made by hand and machine. Molten glass flowed from a furnace through a hollow iron tube called a putny. A worker would cut the stream of molten glass into individual lengths that were then rounded by a machine. In modern marbles, the entire process is mechanized.

"Navarre" is an interesting name. Not only is it the name of a town in Ohio, but it is also the name of a Louisiana bullfighter and an infamous widow.

"Pinpoint Pontil"

Pontil refers to handmade marbles that were made using a punty or pontil. A pontil is a hollow iron rod used to gather molten glass. Molten glass is formed into a glob at the tip of the pontil and rounded into a single marble. Pontils can be identified by the rough mark that the tool leaves on the marble.

As it turns out, "Pontil" is also a fine Italian name, as in diTommaso Pontil or Massimiliano Pontil.

"Cat's Eye"

Marble King was one of the first companies to produce cat's eye marbles in the United States. It began in the mid-fifties in an attempt to compete with imported marbles from Japan. Since then Marble King has established cat's eyes as a standard for every marble collection.

"Cat" is also a wonderful nickname for any of a number of Cathys, Katelyns, Catherines, et al. It's also the last name of a person in the Los Angeles phone book – fancy that!

Dian de Wolf

Dian was born in Bakersfield, California in 1940. She graduated in 1963 with
a Bachelor of Arts degree from the California College of Arts and Crafts. Dian
resides in the small town of Sebastopol, California, where she has woven her
art around raising her children and, now, grandchildren. Children with their
fascination for life, the discovery of a seashell or an intimate mother/child
portrait are the subjects of many of her works. Dian's art has appeared in
galleries across Northern California. Her work has also shown in numerous
state and local art festivals where she has received awards for her use of Pen
and Ink and Watercolor. Dian describes the process as, "It's not just art. It is
a commitment to improve myself. Every painting has its own life – or death
and with each one I grow a little." What you see here is the joy of living fully
and the extension of that life in her work."

Richard Neumann

Richard was born in Burbank, California, in 1957, the son of an aerospace
engineer and a Hollywood movie starlet. He graduated from San Jose State
in 1979 with a Bachelor of Science degree in Business. Although his career has
taken him down the path of corporate CFO, his love has always been writing.
Richard spent a good portion of his high school years writing and produc-
ing amateur movies and working backstage for local theaters. Years later he
returned to writing and the theater as ways to bring tranquility to the turmoil
of high-stress corporate mergers and acquisitions. He has completed two full-
length novels and is deep into a third – as yet unpublished. Richard has also
written five stage plays, three of which have been produced. Recently, one
of his editorials about surviving corporate layoffs appeared in the Santa Rosa
Press Democrat.